CARIN BERGER

OK GO

Greenwillow Books, *An Imprint of HarperCollins Publishers*

GO!

go! go! go!

GO! GO! GO! GO! GO! GO! GO

GO!GO!GO!GO!GO!GO!GO!

STO

e-e-c-h!

SAVE THE PLANET, JANET

RIDE A BIKE, MIKE AND IKE

TAKE A HIKE, SPIKE

THINK GREEN, IRENE

TAKE IT SLOW, JOE

DOUBLE (TRIPLE, QUADRUPLE) UP, PUP

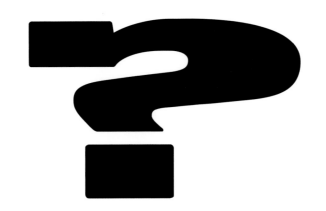

OK GO!

PLANT A TREE, MARIE

USE A TRASH CAN, STAN

SMELL THE POSIES, ROSY

USE IT AGAIN, JEN

CONSERVE, MERVE

RECYCLE, MICHAEL

USE THE BUS, GUS

KEEP IT CLEAN, GENE

I KNOW!

Recycling is finding a new use for something instead of throwing it away.

The collages in this book are made with recycled materials: found papers, magazines, ticket stubs, old letters, and newspapers were used in the art.

To Anya, Jesse, and Willa, so new to this world, and to all of those who work to make it a better, fairer, and more hopeful place. And, as always, with ever expanding love, to Thea

OK Go. Copyright © 2009 by Carin Berger. All rights reserved. Manufactured in China. For information address HarperCollins Children's Books, a division of HarperCollins Publishers, 10 East New York, NY 10022. www.harpercollinschildrens.com. Collages were used to prepare the full-color art. The text type is Franklin Gothic and Black Oak. Library of Congress Publication Data. Berger, Carin. OK go / by Carin Berger. p. cm. "Greenwillow Books." Summary: In this almost wordless picture book, car drivers stuck in traffic under smoggy skies se alternatives to driving, including riding bicycles, walking, and playing. ISBN 978-0-06-157666-9 (trade bdg.) — ISBN 978-0-06-157669-0 (lib. bdg.) [1. Environmental protection— Fiction. 2. Green Fiction. 3. Automobile driving—Fiction.] I. Title. II. Title: Okay go PZ7.B451340k 2009 [E]—dc22 2008014681 09 10 11 12 13 LEO 10 9 8 7 6 5 4 3 First Edition

RECYCLE AND REUSE IT!
Draw on both sides of your paper
*
Make art with old magazines, papers, and boxes
(the illustrations in this book use recycled paper!)
*
Help recycle
*
Donate or trade your used toys and clothes
*
Get books from the library
*
Use only what you need

TURN IT OFF!
Turn off the lights
when you leave a room
*
Turn off the water when
you brush your teeth
*
Read a book instead
of watching TV

YOU CAN DO IT!
Clean up trash
*
Ride your bike or walk
*
Plant a tree

LOOK IT UP! Check out these books and web sites to get more information on how you can help take care of the environment. BOOKS: *Recycle! A Handbook for Kids*, by Gail Gibbons; *Where Does the Garbage Go?*, by Paul Showers; *A Kid's Guide to How to Save the Planet*, by Billy Goodman; *Why Should I Recycle?*, by Jen Green; *Earth Book for Kids: Activities to Help Heal the Environment*, by Linda Schwartz; *50 Simple Things Kids Can Do to Save the Earth*, by John Javna and Michelle Montez. WEB SITES: pbskids.org/zoom/activities/action/way04.html, www.meetthegreens.org